Outside Edge

Neil Hanley

Published in 2016 by FeedARead.com Publishing

Copyright © The author as named on the book cover.

A CIP catalogue record for this title is available from the British Library.

Illustrated by Stephen Turner

Lewis lunged forward and dropped gracefully onto one knee, perfectly balanced. He'd watched the ball carefully all the way. When the time was right, he switched his hands on the grip and swung the bat hard. They weren't expecting it. The fielders were already looking for the ball in the opposite direction. A reverse sweep: four runs.

Twelve-year-old Lewis Duckworth allowed himself a little smile. He finally had the chance to show them all. Not just for his sake, but for his family too. The Duckworth name had been dragged through the mud too many times. Finally, it was time to step up to the plate. Make them all feel proud for once.

And that shot felt good.

He wiped the front of his T-shirt to soak up the sweat and settled into his stance again. He faced side-on, feet slightly apart, bat poised inches off the ground. Perfectly balanced, waiting.

At the other end, Kingswood Manor's fast bowler and main threat was preparing to run in.

'Right, I've had enough of this.' Josh Inglewood scowled. 'No one makes me look stupid. I'll wipe his dirty little nose with this – just watch.'

Inglewood winked at a teammate, gave the ball one last rub, positioned the seam across his fingers and pushed off.

Lewis stood totally still, his eyes fixed on the incoming runner. It was the final school cricket match of term. At last he had been given the chance to play for Parkside's first eleven. He wanted to shove all the bad words ever aimed at him back down everyone's throat.

Mr Feltham, umpiring at the bowler's end, and Parkside's sports teacher knew it had been a risk. The other teachers had frowned at his decision. But he had seen something special in the boy during net practice. He deserved a chance. He just prayed he wouldn't let them down.

Inglewood arrived at the wicket with a sharp grunt and let fly. The ball dug hard and fast into the sun-scorched turf. It was too fast for Lewis, and caught him flat-footed. It swung wickedly towards him and his head jerked back. The ball fizzed passed the edge of his bat, shooting within inches of his nose.

Then came the shrill, 'HOWZAT!' a sound Lewis didn't want to hear. He managed to keep his balance and flashed a look behind him. The ball was sandwiched between the keeper's thick red-and-white gloves. Lewis held his breath. That was never going to be out. He thought he'd done well just to avoid it. As he turned to face the white-coated figure of Mr Feltham, his worst fears came true. He raised the dreaded index finger for everyone to see.

It stopped Lewis dead in his tracks. He couldn't believe it.

Inglewood jumped up and down, slapping high fives to just about everyone on the pitch. His celebration was way over the top. He started to taunt Lewis as he made his way down towards him.

'Better hop off, you're staining the wicket.' Inglewood began to laugh, then stopped suddenly, seeing Lewis hadn't moved. 'Are you blind as well as thick? You're out!'

'I'm not out, I didn't touch it!' Lewis protested.

'The umpire's decision is final – kindly leave the the field,' Mr Feltham said with a slight annoyance.

Inglewood was in his face.

'Hey, Stig! Shove off! Accept it, you're out!'

'I'll shove this bat down your throat if you don't shut it.' Lewis had lost his cool. He'd been warned about his temper, but he'd had enough of these taunts. Rage burned inside him. Mr Feltham didn't really want him to do well. No one did. Well, he didn't care any more.

Inglewood continued to pull faces at him and pointed towards the pavilion, enraging Lewis even further.

'You're stinking out the wicket.' He turned to a teammate and smirked. 'All the same, that lot from the

King's estate – you can smell 'em a mile off.'

Lewis snapped. Nothing else mattered now. Inglewood had crossed the line. The bat was now a weapon, and Lewis turned and began waving it at Inglewood. He would have smashed it over his silly head if the opposition fielder hadn't charged into him, pushing him sideways onto the grass.

'Get off me!' Lewis shouted.

He pushed the fielder roughly away and rolled onto his side. It was then that he heard yowls and slaps, and turned see what was happening. Inglewood was being attacked by Lewis' older brothers Charlie and Walter. Charlie was aiming wild blows in all directions and Inglewood's nose was bleeding. Lewis' heart sank. He knew he was in deep trouble.

'Pack it in! Enough!' barked Mr Feltham, trying to

step between Charlie and Inglewood.

They took no notice. Charlie threw the next blow when Walter came charging in, pinning Inglewood to the ground. He didn't stand a chance against his brother's stocky frame. Another of Inglewood's teammates joined in, hammering on Walter's back. Then it was all over.

The headmaster Mr Tanner bulldozed his way through the pile of bodies, dragging both Charlie and Walter away. Inglewood got to his feet shakily, wiping blood from his nose. Mr Feltham straightened his coat. He was red faced and pointed sharply at Lewis.

'OFF! Now! Get changed. Go straight to Mr Tanner's office! That's the last time you'll ever play for The school team.'

Lewis trudged off, dragging his bat behind him in

disgrace. He couldn't believe what had just happened. As he walked off, he looked up to see a red Transit van parked up on the boundary edge. His brothers must have skipped off work early to come along and watch him play.

The Duckworths had just turned a cricket match into a boxing contest; things were worse than ever.

2

His friend Matt was padding up when he got back to the changing room. He looked surprised to see him.

'Hey! You okay?'

'I'm fine,' said Lewis as he struggled with a buckle.

His head was thumping. He could still feel the heat radiating from his forehead without even touching it.

'Look at the state of you. What happened?'

'Feltham gave me out, but I wasn't … I didn't touch it.'

Lewis flung his bat into the school kit bag, ripped off the last pad and sat down. He looked at himself in

the mirror. Matt was right, he was in a state. His black curly hair was full of dead grass and his once white T-shirt was now a shade of brown. There was even a small rip in his crumpled white jeans. He didn't even have the right gear. He must have looked a right joke.

'Are you sure you're okay?' Matt could see his friend was livid.

Lewis finally looked up.

'That's it, Matt, I've blown it.'

'It can't be that bad – it wasn't a goldie, was it?'

'No, no.' He sighed. 'It's not that... I got into a fight, then my brothers turned up. It turned into a big scrap. Old Tanner got involved. I've got to go and see him. My match is finished.'

Matt gave a low whistle.

'Feltham's banned me from playing for the school,

too.'

'That's his loss! Well anyway, end of term, isn't it? Soon be forgotten about.'

'I doubt it.'

Lewis slumped forward. Clapping and cheering could be heard through the open window.

Matt grabbed his bat and gloves.

'Oh no! That's nine down, I'm in!'

Just before he left, he turned to Lewis.

'Look, why don't you take me up on the offer, come with me to nets on Tuesday evening at Clifton? We're always looking for new players. You never know, you might get a game – you're good enough. Forget about the school team. I know I have, batting me this far down the order.'

Lewis forced a smile. Matt never seemed

bothered by what others thought about their friendship. He liked him just because of it. The door clicked shut and Matt was gone. Lewis was left alone with his thoughts. He still couldn't believe what had happened earlier.

Ever since his family arrived in town six months ago, it was the same old story. When the Duckworths had arrived in Westburn with not much money, there was only one place they could stay: Kings Country Park, an estate full of chalets and condominiums.

But it wasn't a very nice place. It was just off the main carriageway on the edge of town. It wasn't very clean and the locals attributed it to the rise in crime. The police were regularly on patrol.

It had been his fourth school in as many years. Every time his dad would lose their rented home through a lack of work. This would frustrate his father, who was so desperate to fit in and do well. Lewis dreaded him knowing about this. Instead, he wished he could go home and tell him how well he'd done.

By the time Lewis had changed and reached the door, he could hear the chatter of voices and the clatter of boots echoing through the pavilion. Their innings had finished.

Lewis kicked the back door open and stomped out. He wanted to avoid his so-called teammates. He felt ashamed, but most of all angry with himself. He'd expected so much of himself in the match but he had delivered nothing.

He should have been happy; after all, it was the end of term and the start of the school holidays. But as he made his way reluctantly to the headmaster's office,

he just felt sick with dread.

3

'You disappoint me, Duckworth, I thought you were different. Violence has no place at my school, especially on the cricket field. As for your brothers, if I ever catch them on school property again, I'll call the police.'

The door opened to Mr Tanner's office and in came the school secretary, Mrs Brown. Her face was flushed. She handed Mr Tanner a letter and with several short, quick strides scuttled back out. She was always in a hurry. She still found the time to scowl at Lewis, though. Lewis felt empty inside.

Mr Tanner reached for a pen and continued to speak to him while he wrote something on a piece of paper.

'You know full well you have to try harder than anyone else at this school to convince me I made the right choice letting you in. Your track record so far hasn't exactly been glowing. On a couple of occasions you have been caught fighting.'

He put down the pen and began folding the letter.

'If you wanted to take up boxing, you only had to ask. I'd be quite happy to pull on the gloves again. A few rounds with me and you won't know what's hit you.'

Lewis couldn't believe what he was hearing. One minute he was telling him violence was bad, the next he was almost encouraging it. It was as if Mr Tanner had read his mind.

'Boxing is a sport, by the way; controlled

aggression, not the mindless violence I saw earlier.'

He stuffed the letter into an envelope and passed it across the desk to Lewis.

'Take this home to your father. He seems a reasonable man, I'm sure he'll understand. Now get out of here.'

It felt so unfair. He wasn't a violent child. Two fights in two terms wasn't that bad. He just wished he wouldn't get so mad about the insults.

Just as he was about to open the door, Mr Tanner spoke again.

'Oh, and one other thing do yourself a favour before you go, see your teammates and apologise for letting them down. You've got a lot to learn, Duckworth; things like sportsmanship and playing for the team. I've heard you're quite good, too. Pity.'

A fleeting sadness crossed Mr Tanner's face. Lewis found himself staring. Mr Tanner straightened up.

'Now get out of my office!'

4

'Hey, son, you're 'ome early,' Jack Duckworth said as soon as he reached the front step.

He was standing at the door. The top half could be opened separately, so all Lewis could see was his dad's suntanned face as he mounted the two steps to the chalet.

'Finished early, didn't it.'

Lewis pushed open the bottom door and eased past his dad's bulky frame. He didn't feel like saying much. His dad wouldn't understand anyway. He didn't know anything about cricket.

'Didn't expect you, that's all – got me'self some company.'

23

Lewis looked across into the dimly lit corner. Squashed into the curved red sofa were three suited men. They were unsmiling and looked hot, their red sunburnt faces glistening against the reflection of the window.

The fattest of the three and nearest to Lewis said, 'And who's this?'

'This is one of my sons, Lewis.'

The skinniest man in the far corner scribbled some notes onto a pad.

'He's no trouble – fitted in well round here. He's just played for his school's cricket team, in't that right eh, son?'

He looked proudly at Lewis, who felt even worse now. He prayed his dad wouldn't ask him any questions about the match. He hated lying.

'These people are from the housing department at

the council, Lewis. They're kindly helping get us on the council list for our own place, and the Duggans next door.'

Lewis had seen it all before. Dad had tried many times to, as he liked to call it, 'go to work with the council', but had always failed. Lewis supposed he wanted to be friends with them. Perhaps this time would be different. They looked at Lewis with an air of caution and suspicion. Lewis immediately felt uncomfortable.

'Dad, I'm tired. I'm going to have a rest in my room, is that okay?'

'Sure, we'll catch up later. Mum'll be back soon for dinner.'

Lewis crossed the room, heading for the side door. He glimpsed his baby brother Carl on the floor. Knelt beside him was Aisha Duggan. She loved looking after Carl. They were sat in front of the cold grey coal fire playing with his toys.

He opened the door, finding himself outside for a moment. Two small steps led to another door and a small chalet opposite. Once inside, he was relieved to find the bedroom empty.

He slumped onto his bed and let out a big sigh. He still felt a twinge of anger and frustration. He hadn't gone back to his teammates as Mr Tanner had asked him to. They weren't even his mates. Everyone had practically ignored him, apart from Matt.

Outside he could hear the Duggan children playing and their dog Chico barking. He flicked on the radio. It was nearly time for the final session of play on day one of the second test at Lord's. And then all the sounds outside would disappear. He loved hearing the commentators. He would leave his chalet life behind and become the batsman facing the next delivery.

He shared his bedroom within the small chalet with his older brothers. He tried to make his small section of the room feel like his own, putting up posters of his favourite cricket stars and stacking over a hundred second-hand cricket magazines neatly on his bedside cabinet.

His whole family prided themselves on being neat and tidy, yet the TV still needed fixing. At least the radio worked.

Then he remembered the letter in his back pocket.

5

As he turned the letter over in his hand he thought about what he should do. Perhaps he should give it to his dad. No, not in front of those people from the council; that wouldn't look good, would it? So what if he didn't give it to him at all? It would be another two months before school started again. Like Matt said, it would all be forgotten by then.

He quickly opened the letter and began to read.

Dear Mr Duckworth,

I am writing to inform you that your son, Lewis, one of my pupils in Year 7, has been banned forthwith from playing on the school cricket team after a bad display of sportsmanship during the game with

Kingswood Manor today, when Lewis

started a fight.

I won't tolerate violence at my school. This

has already caused us deep embarrassment

and I fear it may jeopardise our future

relations with Kingswood.

I recall our first meeting before Christmas

when you assured me that I could trust you

and your family implicitly. You told me at

the time that you were looking for

permanent accommodation after several

bad breaks in recent years.

'Don't worry, you can trust our Lewis, he's

different,' you said. 'He won't cause you

any trouble.' Well, today I completely lost

that trust. His behaviour on the cricket field was a disgrace. As I'm told it's the first time that he has crossed the line, this shall be a warning to him. My school has an excellent reputation for teaching young people the skills needed to help them achieve in life. I won't allow standards to slip.

Any repeat of aggression towards teachers or pupils and I will have no hesitation in expelling him, which may have a bearing on your family's future in this town.

Can I offer some advice to young Lewis? If you are reading this letter to him now I would like you to tell him that on the sports field he has much to learn about sportsmanship and playing in a team. You

have to accept a decision from an official as

final and walk away graciously. I hate to

see good talent wasted. Perhaps it would be

good that he spends this summer 'usefully'.

I'm sure you know what is best for your son

and your family. And I know what is best

for my school.

Yours sincerely

Mr Tanner, Headteacher, Parkside

Comprehensive

Lewis read it again and again. There were some big

words that he didn't understand, but he got the drift. He

hadn't even mentioned his brothers. It wasn't fair.

Though he was glad he'd read it first; his dad would

have blown his top. Mr Tanner was actually threatening

his father. He read the last paragraph again. He slipped

the letter back into his pocket. He had a pretty good

idea about what to do now. He knew he had another

crack at it, and he was going to give it everything

he had.

6

At six-thirty on Tuesday evening Lewis was out in the yard. His mum had wanted his help with the washing. She had arranged it all in a large basket and was hanging it out to dry in the yard, huffing and puffing. Lewis hated doing chores. He had spent the last half an hour playing catch against a corrugated shed, much to his mum's annoyance. His old tennis ball would bounce off in all directions. It sharpened his skills and acted as a good warm-up for tonight's cricket practice.

The sound of Chico barking alerted Lewis to the front entrance. Matt stood outside, shifting his long bag awkwardly around his body. He had agreed to meet Lewis on his way to Clifton Park. Lewis didn't have any kit to carry. He wore the same T-shirt and white jeans from the week before. They were clean of course, and his mum had repaired the rip in his jeans; he told them he got it going for a diving catch. He had made up things about last week's match. His dad seemed to accept it; he had no reason not to. His brothers had feigned interest, but he could see them smirking. He hoped that would be the end of it. He would help mum with the chores later. All he wanted to do now was play cricket.

They set off for the park. Matt was quite clever. He was in all the top sets at school. Perhaps if he had been out in the middle and able to calm Lewis down, everything would have been different. He might still have only got four runs with the bat, but he could have shown them how he could field. He loved fielding almost as much as batting.

Halfway through their walk to Clifton Park, Lewis suddenly came to a halt.

'What's up?' Matt asked, curious.

'Matt,' Lewis began tentatively, 'what if they all hate me?'

'So? Has that really bothered you before?'

'I want to fit in.'

'Don't worry, once they see you play you'll fit right in.'

'But what if it's like the school match?'

'It'll be okay. Anyway, I heard that you did well to get out of the way of that ball. Most people would have got hit or run a mile. You stood up to it. You didn't flinch. You'll be fine.'

'Matt, can I ask you something else?'

'Yes, what is it?'

'Are there … umm, do you think I could…?' he stammered. 'Is there somewhere I could shower afterwards?'

'Shower? Yes, but none of us use them.'

'Could *I* use them?'

Lewis felt a wave of embarrassment. It was awkward with no shower at home and his family unable to afford baths every day. He hated feeling dirty.

'Listen,' Matt said, sizing him up; he was a foot shorter, with blonde hair that came to just below Lewis' chin. 'Don't worry about a thing. You can have a shower if you want after practice. So can we go and play some cricket and show them how good you are?'

'Yeah, cool,' said Lewis, doing his best to force a smile.

7

By the time Lewis and Matt arrived, Clifton Maiden's Under-13s squad was already warming up. The practice nets were a flurry of activity. The regular 'clack' of bat against ball could be heard across the park as families strolled in the evening sun.

Lewis felt nervous. He followed like a puppy dog as Matt dumped his bag and joined four boys huddled together at the back of one of the nets. They talked about anything and everything except cricket. Only when it was time to bowl did they screw their faces up in quiet concentration as they prepared to run in.

'This is Lewis,' Matt announced.

'All right,' said a chubby boy in the middle of the

group.

The rest just nodded coolly. Lewis sensed it straight away. He'd seen the look a hundred times before. Something in their eyes gave it away. Was it fear, or hatred? He saw them looking at his jeans and T-shirt. It felt like being at school all over again.

The chubby boy broke into a smile. He seemed more welcoming.

'What are you then? A batter or a bowler?' he asked.

'Err, I like batting and *fielding* actually.'

'You like fielding? Urrgh! That's *so* boring.'

'That's because you'd rather stand in the slips picking your nose, Patterson! You should get your lardy backside running about like the rest of us,' one of the boys joked.

The other three sniggered.

'Hey, take that back.'

The boy known as Patterson may have been on the tubby side, but he showed his strength as he pulled the other boy into a headlock.

'They're only messing,' said Matt, sensing Lewis' unease.

'Hey, Patterson, Blake, pack it in. You know the rules at practice, no mucking about in the nets!'

Patterson and Blake stopped what they were doing. The voice had come from down the far end. Lewis saw a smartly dressed boy, pointing his bat in their direction. Then he resumed his poise, ready to face the next delivery. He wore a helmet, his white pads glistening; he looked like a pro. Lewis had to watch.

Perfectly balanced, the boy rose up onto his toes and smashed the ball back in their direction. Patterson and Blake jumped out of the way.

'See!' he called out. 'Don't muck about or you'll get hurt.'

'Who's that?' asked Lewis.

'Oh, that's our captain, Westlake, biggest mouth at the club,' said Matt. 'Best player, though,' he added.

Lewis was mesmerised.

His session over, Westlake walked towards them. He gave Lewis a fleeting glance, then stopped and frowned.

'Christ, what happened to wearing proper gear at practice?'

Lewis flushed a deep red. He felt everyone staring at him.

Patterson spoke up. 'Oh belt up, Westlake! You think you can boss us lot about just 'cos Coach Riley isn't here.'

'Who's padded up in this net, anyone?' Westlake asked, ignoring him.

No one put themselves forward.

'Well? Come on, someone!'

Westlake turned to look at Lewis again. He looked him up and down and jabbed his bat in his direction.

'You,' he said.

'Me?' said Lewis.

'Yes you, you're next. Get padded up!'

His first test. Sooner than expected.

8

Lewis soon realised why everyone had kept so quiet. The wicket was dodgy. No one was that keen to bat on it, apart from Westlake it seemed. His hands shook nervously as he prepared himself. He desperately wanted to make amends for the school match.

The first ball stayed low, and he just managed to dig it out in time. The second one found a divot and struck his gloves. He concentrated hard. He didn't want to get out. Already his hands felt hot and clammy inside his gloves. He trembled and gritted his teeth, adrenaline surging through his body. He wanted to hit everything. He had felt like this the very first time he held a bat two years ago.

He decided that if the ball dropped short he would cross-bat it into the nets. If it was full, he drove it straight and heard the cry of 'Heads!' every time, even though he tried to keep it low. His hands gripped the handle tightly. Sometimes the ball flew off the edge and Lewis cursed. Some of his drives managed to work the ball through a gap in the nets. Then the bowler cursed. Occasionally he missed, especially when he faced Westlake. He was a clever bowler and deceptively quick. Matt was right, he was good.

Westlake knew it, too. Each time he beat him, he would give Lewis a smug look. *Next time*, thought Lewis, *I'll blast him right over the nets*. But he didn't get the chance. His call came.

'Last ball, next batsman ready!'

Head radiated from Lewis' forehead. His shirt

stuck to his back as he played out the last ball. His back ached. Had he impressed? He thought he'd done okay. And where was the coach? His thoughts were on anything except seeing where he was walking. He felt his leg snag against something, and then he lost his balance, pulling the net with him. His pads flapped noisily, the bat flew high in the air and he landed flat on his face.

Lewis closed his eyes. Already he could hear laughter, quiet at first, then roaring howls of derision. He looked up to see the entire squad collapsing in stitches.

Westlake led the chorus. 'WOOAH! Is he trying to wreck what's left of our nets or what?'

They must have seen the whole thing. Lewis felt sick with embarrassment. He didn't know what was worse, this or the school match last week. He had certainly made an impression, but not the kind he was hoping for.

9

'You okay?'

A large hand reached out and pulled Lewis to his feet. His gaze was met by a black face and gleaming white teeth.

'Coach Carlton Riley,' he said in his soft Caribbean tone. 'Don't worry about the net, I'll get someone to straigh'en it.'

Lewis looked at the net, where there was now a gap wide enough to drive a car through.

'Nets have nearly 'ad it anyway and need replacing soon.'

Lewis saw Coach Riley staring at him. He was frowning, but at the same time he smiled.

'Lewis Duckworth, right?'

Lewis nodded.

'From what I saw there, you're hitting the ball well enough. You've got a natural eye … a little raw maybe.'

Lewis sensed him looking at his jeans and T-shirt.

'You play for anyone?'

'Err, no.'

'Good, I'll get you registered with us then. Quarter-finals next week. We're always looking to strengthen our squad. Can you catch?'

'Yeah.'

'Well, get yourself over to the slip cradle with the others. I'll bring the registration papers on Thursday night. Okay?'

'Sure.'

Lewis joined Matt at the slip cradle.

'Nice one, Lewis – told you it'd be okay. You'll be on the team in no time,' Matt said.

'I hope I didn't break the nets falling over them like that.'

'Forget about that.' Matt smiled. 'Though you have to admit it was funny.'

Lewis raised a smile. If he got on the team his dad would be doubly pleased. He'd still think he was in the school team, too. That would make things easier, he was sure of it. It was all about reputation. He promised himself he'd be the best player in the team by the end of the summer.

In the distance he saw Coach Riley heading for the old pavilion. Another man who looked strangely familiar stepped out of a nearby car and walked across to Riley. The man shook hands with him and soon they were deep in conversation.

'Who's that talking with Riley?' Lewis asked.

'It looks like…' Matt's face dropped. 'No way! So it is true then...'

'What's true? What?'

'It's Feltham.'

'Feltham? Impossible! School's finished for the summer. What's *he* doing here?'

'He's not a teacher now, is he, Lewis?' He glanced knowingly at his friend and then looked back at Riley and Feltham. 'He's playing for *us* this season. He's joined our senior team,' he said emphatically.

'No way.' Lewis felt cold inside. He couldn't believe his poor luck.

'Hey, what does it matter? Riley picks the team.

You've got nothing to worry about.'

Lewis said nothing. He didn't feel reassured by Matt's words. He watched them talking, acting like they were good friends. Lewis was sure that the arrival of Feltham had jeopardised his chance of playing. Riley had probably told him already. It was just a matter of time. He might as well give up and go home now.

By the time practice finished Lewis' mood still hadn't lifted. After a quick shower he trudged home in silence alongside Matt, who kept trying to tell him things would be okay, but he couldn't shrug off seeing Mr Feltham. Things were about to get worse as Lewis walked into the yard. His father was waiting by the chalet. Even in the dim light he could see he was angry. Lewis then realised why. His antics at school were about to catch up with him.

Lewis' dad glared at him from across the small table whilst Charlie and Walter leaned casually against the fridge, watching intently. Lewis flinched as his dad waved the letter in front of him. The flimsy paper flapped like a kite in the wind.

'So, were you gonna to tell me about this?'

His dad looked at him with angry eyes. He then slowly read a line from the letter out loud.

'*…I recall our first meeting before Christmas when you assured me that I could trust you and your family implicitly.*'

'But it wasn't *all* my fault,' Lewis pleaded.

He looked across at his brothers. They stood in

stony silence. Their faces gave nothing away, although he swore he could see a hint of a smile from Walter. *Why aren't they saying anything?* Lewis thought to himself.

'I don't want to hear it. You've let the family down big time.'

'But I didn't–'

'I don't want to hear it, Lewis.' His dad fixed his eyes on the letter again, shaking his head. 'Don't you realise that all them lot are after is an excuse, just one excuse to terminate our application and kick us out of here?'

He closed the letter and his eyes. His body started shaking.

'But, Dad, it wasn't my fault.'

'Enough, Lewis!'

Lewis jumped as his dad slammed his fist down on the table.

'Take a look at your brothers. D'ya see any trouble coming from them?'

He pointed to them both. Walter swigged casually from a carton of milk.

'No! They work hard, keep their heads down and their noses clean. They are busting a gut for the family's sake. But *you*, you've got a lot to learn. Seems to me hard work is what you need. You know your mum needs all the help she can get with her health, and it's about time you started pulling your weight around here. I'll make sure you're kept useful. You can help more around the place. Until you start pulling your finger out and helping your mum, no playing cricket!'

'What! No way, that's *so* unfair.'

'I'm sorry; until I can trust you again, you're grounded. That's the end of it.'

Lewis' dad stuffed the letter into his pocket and marched out of the chalet.

'Thanks for your support,' Lewis said, turning his anger towards Charlie and Walter.

Walter put the carton of milk on the table and leaned against Lewis. Lewis could smell his brother's hot milky breath.

'Always best to keep the gob shut, don't want to make it worse, know what I mean, bro?' Walter said.

Lewis jerked his arm away, spilling the carton of milk all over the table.

'You'd better clear that up. You don't want dad to *really* lose his temper.'

Lewis scowled. His dad wasn't the only one who was angry.

His punishment lasted just over a week. During that time his dad hadn't spoken to him. Instead, he left a list of jobs for him to do each day. That meant sweeping the yard, hanging washing, emptying bins and scrubbing floors, practically anything his dad could think of. Most days Lewis wouldn't finish until 9 o'clock at night. Worst of all he'd missed practice and a chance to play in the Inter-Town Twenty Cup. Matt reckoned he would have got into the team, too.

That afternoon as he slaved away sweeping the yard for probably the hundredth time, Lewis' thoughts had turned to running away. That would show them. He had an uncle who lived on the canal. He could stay with him. Lead a quiet life with no one on his back. He could just drift in and out of places. He need never worry about fitting in again.

Then he thought of his mum, struggling with her health. It didn't help what with the car fumes filling her lungs every second of the day and night. That just made her asthma worse. He started feeling guilty for running out to practice the other day. Perhaps he'd been a bit selfish. His dad had a right to have a go at him. He felt a lump in his throat. He wiped away a tear just as his dad came ambling towards him, whistling to himself. He always did that when he was happy about something.

'Okay, you can stop that now,' he said. 'Lewis, great news, the application is going through nicely. We're nearly there. They reckon we have a good chance now. I've got a really good feeling this time.'

Lewis had heard it all before. The rejections followed sooner or later. Then it was just a matter of time before they moved on. It never seemed to get his dad down, though, or if it did he never seemed to show it.

'Look, Lewis,' he said, turning serious for a moment, 'the last thing I want is to ruin your summer holidays, but you have to promise me that you'll help more around here. I don't want to hear about any more trouble. It's a critical time for the family right now. We all need to be pulling in the same direction. Okay?'

He ruffled Lewis' hair with his fat sausage-like fingers. Lewis knew how important this was for his dad. He had set his heart on a house in Medway Fields, a place away from the industrial estates, busy roads and railways. It would mean clean, fresh air with plenty of space, somewhere they could finally call home. For his dad the wait was almost over.

All Lewis wanted to do was make the most of what was left of the summer.

12

Lewis ran towards the pavilion on the far side of Clifton Park. He sprinted straight past a group of boys messing about in the playground. He avoided eye contact. He sensed them watching him like hawks. *Stay away from trouble.* He remembered his dad's warning. He had to concentrate on himself.

Matt was visiting his grandparents, so Lewis was forced to train alone. Still he had with him his trusty tennis ball. Searching beside the nets he picked up an old stump. Perfect. At the back of the old wooden pavilion the ground was hard and flat; *even better*. He didn't need anything else.

He began throwing the ball against the pavilion.

He made it bounce once into his path. He played it away with the old stump. As always when he played alone he soon drifted into his own little world. He started to commentate on himself.

Today it was the second test at Lord's. The ball pinged back off the wall again. This time he played it off his hips.

'Touched away nicely, brings a couple of runs,' he began saying in a low voice. 'First runs of the day, two for no wicket. Bowler returns to his mark. A lovely sunny day here at Lord's, a packed crowd–'

'Lewis?'

He stopped dead in his tracks.

'Lewis Duckworth, is that you?' came the call again.

Lewis held his breath. He turned and saw Coach

Riley walking towards him.

'I saw someone hanging around the pavilion, wasn't sure if you were with them lot over there.'

He pointed towards the group of boys in the playground. 'Who were you talking to?'

'Err … no one.' Lewis flushed a deep red.

'What happened to you last week? I thought you were joining us.'

Lewis felt suddenly awkward for a different reason. 'I'm sorry, Mr Riley, I … I had things to do.'

'Oh.' Coach Riley frowned. He looked disappointed.

'I really wanted to come…'

'Hey, don't worry, no need to explain. What are you doing here now?

Lewis saw him looking at the stump.

63

'I'm … practising.'

'I see…' He rubbed his chin, looking thoughtfully at Lewis. 'On your own?'

'Yeah.'

'Do you want some help?'

'Well…'

'I can give you some coaching, if you like? I've got some time before I drive home.'

'But I've only got an old tennis ball and a stump.'

'It didn't stop *you*, did it? Besides, what I'm going to teach you won't need even a ball. Didn't the lads tell you about Shot Selecta?' Coach Riley grinned, revealing his gleaming white teeth. 'Just wait here, I won't be long.'

As Coach Riley headed for his car, Lewis found himself scratching his head. He had never been properly coached before. What did Coach Riley have in store for him? And what was Shot Selecta all about?

13

'Hold it … keep your balance … hold it. That's it.'

Coach Riley's soft Caribbean voice never ceased. Lewis strained joints and muscles just to hold the shot in position. Coach Riley walked around him. Occasionally he'd adjust Lewis' feet or straighten his head. Lewis felt like a puppet on a string.

'Hold it, Lewis. Okay and relax.'

Lewis blew out his cheeks. He felt a spasm in his thigh.

'Okay, ready to go again. Straight drive…'

Lewis had soon discovered what Shot Selecta was all about. Coach Riley had returned from his car with two cricket bats and a file containing some papers. He'd handed Lewis a bat and without the need for a ball, Coach Riley took him through a vast range of cricket strokes. Some of them he knew, others he'd never tried or heard of before.

He had stretched himself into a full sweep, followed by a back-foot drive, a hook, a cut, a pull and a forward defensive. It went on. Each time he played a stroke he was forced to hold it into position, sometimes for as long as a minute whilst Coach Riley checked his technique. It was agony. Lewis grimaced as he twisted and strained. His body moved into shapes and arcs he'd never thought possible. He struggled at times just to hold his balance. He was allowed to rest for no more than five seconds. He must have been working hard for at least twenty minutes, the sweat shining on his brown arms.

Ten minutes later Coach Riley called the session to a halt. Lewis collapsed to the floor. His back ached and his feet pounded.

'Well done, Lewis. Remember, this will help your balance and concentration, not to mention your flexibility and stamina. All the disciplines you will need to become a good batsman.'

Lewis had been reminded about this throughout the entire session.

'Just wait until you hit a real ball, you'll have all the shots in the book. Next you'll have to learn when to play them,' Coach Riley said, his face breaking into a wide grin.

Lewis had just enough energy to nod. His mouth felt dry. His muscles already felt sore. His hot skin itched against the grass.

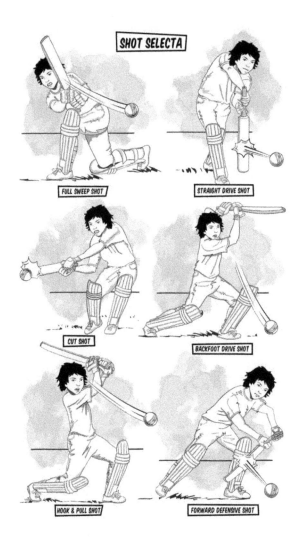

SHOT SELECTA

FULL SWEEP SHOT

STRAIGHT DRIVE SHOT

CUT SHOT

BACKFOOT DRIVE SHOT

HOOK & PULL SHOT

FORWARD DEFENSIVE SHOT

Coach Riley now produced the file. 'Right, now to finally register you.'

Lewis' energy returned and his eyes lit up in that moment.

Coach Riley looked up from the papers spread in his hands.

'I'll need you to be part of our team for next week's semi-final. Don't let me down!'

'What do you think, Lewis, not bad, eh? This is where the final will be played.'

As they went in through the large black-metal gates, Lewis tried to contain his excitement as he saw the sign.

WELCOME TO WESTBURN CRICKET CLUB

He noticed the high walls surrounding the ground. The tarmac car park gave way to the outfield, so perfectly mown it was hard to believe it was made of grass. His white pumps met the spongy green surface. It was like walking on carpet. A tingle went through his body. Images of hitting the winning runs in the final flooded through him. He could see Matt was just as excited.

Up ahead he caught sight of the pavilion. It stood vast and imposing, gleaming white in the sunshine. An impressive balcony lined with deckchairs showed off the large clock above it. Although Lewis didn't dare go inside he could make out the deep-red carpet, and several large signs telling players not to wear spikes in the pavilion. It was a world away from Clifton Park. It was a world away from his chalet home.

Lewis focused on the action out at the wicket. Clifton Seniors' first eleven were batting. Coach Riley glanced the ball elegantly off his hips. At the other end non-striker Mr Feltham broke into a run. Lewis squeezed his lips tight. The sight of Mr Feltham made him feel uneasy. Despite being put in the team for Tuesday night's semi-final, something nagged away at him. But he couldn't put his finger on it.

They met up with the other boys from Clifton huddled close to the nets on the far side of the ground. Westburn's Under-13s were practising in nets that made Clifton's look like rags. The entire bay was tight and firm, like the strings of a guitar. Westlake, Clifton's captain, was talking to a group of boys. He ignored Lewis as he approached.

It was Ben Patterson who greeted them with his usual cheery grin.

'Hey, ready for Tuesday night? Can't wait! Imagine playing here if we win.'

'Who's Westlake talking to?' Lewis asked tentatively.

'Westburn boys – he played for them last season. Fraternising with the enemy,' Patterson said, loud enough so that Westlake could hear.

'Didn't cut the mustard, but came back to us didn't he?' Matt said in a quieter voice. 'Westburn is *the* main club in the town, and they usually nick all the best players.

Even our seniors only play against their reserves.'

'It wasn't just that, Matt,' corrected Patterson. 'I heard he didn't get on with some of the players. Fancy, we could meet Westburn in the final, the holders too.'

Then Lewis heard him. The voice was unmistakable.

'Hey! We don't allow tramps into our ground!'

The insult was aimed at Lewis.

15

Lewis spun round to see a tall boy clad from head to toe in batting gear walking aggressively towards him.

'What are you doing here?' he demanded.

'Leave us alone, Inglewood. We're not doing any harm. We've every right to be here,' Patterson said, puffing out his chest.

Matt looked uneasily at Lewis, whose face flushed a deep red, his hands rolled into tight fists.

Inglewood went on. 'We don't allow hooligans at our club – clear off.' He hesitated slightly when he saw Lewis standing firm. 'We don't want any trouble.'

Lewis saw that Inglewood couldn't resist a sideways look, as if he was half-expecting Lewis' brothers to come bursting out of nowhere like before. One thing was for sure, thought Lewis to himself, he hadn't forgotten. The other boys had stopped practising. Very soon several players from each side had formed a line facing one another. It was like a stand-off in a western.

Matt whispered hurriedly into Patterson's ear.

'If you're still here when I've finished batting, Duckworth, there'll be trouble,' said Inglewood.

Inglewood retreated and players from both sides dispersed. He bellowed instructions to his fellow players to set up the bowling machine. Lewis stood still. He was pleased he hadn't reacted.

Westlake, however, had seen everything and sidled up to Matt.

'What was all that about with Inglewood?'

'Oh nothing, you know Inglewood.'

'Lewis had a fight with him at school, tried to knock his head off,' Patterson blurted out, much to Matt's disgust, who elbowed him on the arm. 'Argh! What?'

Lewis saw Westlake's eyes narrow. He stared hard at him. Lewis wanted no trouble. *Just leave things as they are*, he thought.

Matt knew this too. 'Come on, Lewis, let's go,' he said.

Before Matt could pull Lewis away, Westlake had his arm on his shoulder.

'You know something? I don't like that Inglewood either.'

Lewis tensed. It was the first time Westlake had bothered to speak to him, and now he was acting like they were good mates.

'What do you reckon, fancy getting your own back?'

Matt shot Lewis a warning look.

'Come on, Lewis, follow me. Just for a laugh, you know what I mean.'

Westlake walked casually towards the bowling machine, urging Lewis to follow. Lewis knew he should walk away. Whatever Westlake had in mind, he could only see trouble ahead. Trouble he desperately wanted to avoid.

16

It was known affectionately as 'The Jug'. Two rotating rubber wheels set on top of three metal legs. The wheels could be adjusted to alter the ball's pitch length, direction and speed. The operator would raise a hand and shout a warning to the batsman before the ball was pushed between the spinning wheels.

Inglewood heard the shout. He knew he would have less than a second to react. He knew that the ball would be full length at a reasonable speed so he could practise his straight drives. Something he wasn't very good at. He leant forward in anticipation. He heard the familiar dull hum and pop as the ball was spat out at him. In a tenth of a second it was all over.

The ball had become a red bullet, descending sharply and hitting the ground with a force he'd never faced before. It rose like a rocket and hit his helmet before he even had time to react. The Jug wasn't being very affectionate. It had just delivered a ball in excess of seventy miles an hour. Inglewood fell like he'd been shot.

'JOSH!' cried the boy standing by The Jug.

He raced to help Inglewood, who lay on the ground in a crumpled heap.

Lewis had watched in horror like the rest of them. He heard Westlake laughing next to him. There was movement at the far end and Inglewood got shakily to his feet.

Lewis could just hear the other boy saying,

'It wasn't me; someone must have tampered with the

machine!'

Inglewood had taken off his helmet. He rubbed the side of his head vigorously. Luckily for him it had been a glancing blow. Luckily too that he'd been wearing a helmet. Next minute he was walking unsteadily towards Lewis. He hadn't even noticed Westlake laughing.

'YOU!' he pointed at Lewis. 'You … you could have killed me!'

'Now hang on a sec, I didn't–'

'Hey, Inglewood, so what? He got you back for last time,' Westlake said before Lewis had a chance to explain.

He turned to Lewis, putting his fingers to his lips.

'Not a word, not a word. Let's wind him up, shall we?'

'But…'

Lewis then realised he'd been duped. Earlier Westlake's slight of hand had changed the speed and direction of The Jug. No one had seen him do it apart from Lewis. Now he'd just made Lewis the culprit without even trying. It seemed Westlake didn't like him, almost as much as Inglewood.

Lewis felt rage starting to build in the pit of his stomach. He fought to control the urge to lash out. Even though Inglewood still looked a little groggy, he'd made ground, despite attempts from teammates to hold him back. He was now inches from Lewis' face.

'Come on then!' he said, goading Lewis. 'You want a fight? This time let's make it fair, one on one.'

'I didn't do anything!'

He'd had enough. Lewis lashed out. He caught the helmet Inglewood had been clutching in his hand. It flew at the boy who had been trying to hold Inglewood back and caught him square above the eye. Matt pulled Lewis away before Inglewood had a chance to retaliate.

'You've done it this time, Duckworth!'

Inglewood tried to move in closer, but his teammates dragged him back. They had the same idea as Matt. They didn't want any trouble either.

'Pack it in, Lewis!' said Matt as he led him further away.

Lewis could hear the threats still coming from Inglewood.

'That's it, you chicken – go back to your stinking hole. You and your family have had it in this town, I'll make sure of that.'

Lewis tensed, pushing against Matt.

'Lewis, that's enough, please!'

Westlake was watching with quiet amusement. The other players from both sides looked on in shock. Someone assisted the boy with the cut eye.

'Let's hope no one saw that,' Matt said, looking around the ground nervously.

The flare-up had lasted no more than a minute. As they made their way along the boundary, Lewis couldn't help but look across at the match. Out at the wicket Mr Feltham leant against his bat during a lull in play.

Even from a distance Lewis could tell he was being watched.

A small crowd had gathered on a warm, sunny evening at Downside Cricket Club. Clifton Maidens' opening pair of Johnson and Parks made their way to the wicket amidst the gentle sound of clapping. Downside's Under-13s took their positions on the field. The Inter-Town Twenty Semi-Final was underway.

Sitting alone on a bench beside the pavilion, Lewis kicked the ground in frustration. He seemed to be the only one who wasn't happy that evening. Coach Riley's idea of him being in the team had been very different to Lewis'. He was supposed to be part of the action, not sitting on the sidelines.

Lewis had been made twelfth man. That was what

Coach Riley had meant all along, *part of the team*. He should have expected it. Did he really think he'd just waltz into the starting line-up? This was a winning team, after all. He couldn't expect Coach Riley to change that. But there was something else. Mr Feltham. Had he got something to do with this?

He was sure Feltham had seen the incident at Westburn and put two and two together. He'd probably told Coach Riley. That's why he'd been relegated to twelfth man. Lewis felt cheated. He was fed up of being blamed for things he hadn't done.

When they warmed up at the start he just felt out of it. Hardly anyone noticed him. Coach Riley had told him that a twelfth man's duty was an important one. Was that meant to make him feel better? General dogs-body more like. Fetching and carrying, that's all he was good for. He considered leaving there and then. Yet he kept reminding himself that after all that had happened, he was still in the squad. That was something to cling onto at least. There was still a chance. So he stayed.

Lewis watched through gritted teeth as Clifton posted an impressive total. Downside needed 152 to win from their allotted twenty overs. The Maidens took to the field. Lewis had hardly moved in two hours; so much for being twelfth man. Coach Riley shouldn't have bothered. He wouldn't be needed today.

Halfway through Downside's innings something happened that changed all that.

By all accounts it should never have happened. The batsman hadn't run wide enough and never looked where he was going. He'd been too busy ball watching.

Crunch! Clifton's wicket keeper, Andy Drake, and Downside's opening batsman collided at the crease. Or rather Downside's batsman ran into him. Andy Drake would have been okay to carry on except he'd fallen awkwardly onto his ankle.

'Duckworth!'

Lewis received the call from Westlake. He jumped quickly to his feet. He tried to shake off the feeling of pins and needles as he struggled to take off his sweatshirt; called into action so suddenly, his legs were trembling and he felt weak. His heart pounded in his throat. This was it. It wasn't exactly how he'd imagined it, but at last he had a chance to show them.

Lewis soon realised how much Westlake hated him. Any chance of receiving the ball would be hopeless. He stuck him on the boundary in a position known as Long On directly behind the bowler. Yet he was bowling to his field, which mostly gathered square-on each side of the wicket. Almost every ball was short of a length. Any chance of driving one straight back seemed remote. At the end of the over Westlake directed Lewis to the opposite end. Lewis had the longest walk of anyone else in the team.

Yet he didn't walk, he ran.

'Come on, lads, keep it tight!' Lewis called out. He couldn't contain himself any longer.

It would be a tight finish. Downside had scored quickly. They had lost more wickets, but they were up on the run rate. With five overs left they needed thirty runs to win. Lewis calculated quickly in his head. That would mean a run a ball. The Maidens were in danger of losing, and Lewis couldn't do a thing about it. He had been on the field for twenty minutes and still hadn't touched the ball. He was itching to get into the action.

Then there it was. The ball was thumped back in a rare front drive that passed by the lunging bowler. The outfield was bumpy. The ball bounced towards Lewis. He went to meet it.

'Come on, Duckworth, get it in – they're running two!' Westlake's voice thundered above everyone else's.

Lewis would have been okay if he hadn't looked

up at Westlake. In a fraction of a second he'd taken his eyes off the ball, allowing it to slip underneath his body. He watched in agony as it hit the boundary rope.

Lewis closed his eyes. He couldn't believe it. He felt every one of his teammates staring at him. The last thing he wanted to do was make things worse.

Westlake couldn't contain himself. 'Come on! We can't afford mistakes now – tighten up! Concentrate, Duckworth!'

'Forget about it, Lewis, head up. Ignore Westlake,' Matt said, trying to console him.

It didn't make him feel much better. Lewis swore to himself. He'd allowed Westlake to get to him and lost concentration at the vital second. He wanted to make amends. He willed the ball in his direction. Downside needed just eight runs to win with one wicket in hand and two overs to get it. All looked lost.

The Downside batsman was feeling confident now. He wanted to end the match in style. In the next over he got his opportunity. He danced down the wicket to a slower delivery and tried to smash it over the bowler's head. This time Lewis heard the batsman swear. The angle of his body looked all wrong. He was stretching and off balance. The dull thud told Lewis he'd mistimed it. It went high in the air over the bowler's head. Lewis had already started to run.

'Lewis'!' he called out.

The ball was dipping fast. He had to sprint to make up the ground. He launched himself into the air, sliding his hands underneath the ball just before it hit the ground. With one hand he gripped the ball. He wasn't about to let go for anything. He slid forwards on his chest, tasting dirt in his mouth. He couldn't even see the

ball now. But he still felt it in his hand.

Matt later described it as the 'catch of the season'.

20

He had been watching from a distance for some time. There was a reason for turning up. He couldn't take his eyes off the boy as the Clifton players left the pitch in celebration. It was the white jeans and T-shirt, not the dark complexion and curly black hair, that made him distinct from his teammates.

He couldn't see his face from where he was standing, but he imagined it wore a broad smile. True it had been a great catch. To run twenty metres in from the boundary and dive forwards at the ball had been a brave thing to do.

He squeezed his hands into tight fists and shoved them into his pocket. He couldn't hide it much longer.

His face hardened, a deep frown etched across it. He couldn't stand it any more.

He turned and walked quickly and purposefully out of the ground.

21

Lewis could see the headlines in the Westburn Gazette already.

Duckworth wonder catch wins match for the Maidens

Lewis had been dropped off on the edge of Clifton Park and was now making his way home alone. Matt was staying on the other side of town with his grandparents, so Lewis had to be content with reliving the moment of the catch on his own. He smiled. His dad would be pleased. It might even help his case for getting the house he wanted.

Lewis was so immersed in his own thoughts that he hadn't even noticed the transit van pull up on the kerb behind him. It was only hearing his name that made him turn around.

'Hey, Lewis!'

Lewis saw Walter hanging out of the window, waving furiously. In the light of the street lamp he could just make out Charlie in the passenger seat. As he drew closer he saw the square-jawed Duggan cousins of Pete and Mickey huddled behind.

'You were miles away, Lewis. What you up to?'

'Walking home … what does it look like?'

Lewis was still cross with Walter and Charlie over the letter business.

Walter chose to ignore Lewis' sharpness. 'Have you seen any kids come through here?' he asked, frowning.

Lewis could see even in the poor light that Charlie twitched in his seat, looking about warily. He saw the dour faces of the Duggan cousins. Usually when he travelled in their van it meant wild singing and lots of laughter, but not this evening. Something was up. Lewis shook his head.

'Some kids chucked stones through our chalet window,' Charlie said. 'They were last seen heading through the park. If we catch 'em...'

Lewis detected the menace in his tone. No one messed with Charlie. A bloody nose would be the result, as Inglewood had found out. This was a direct attack on the family.

'Is everyone okay?'

'Mum's shaken up. Best you get home right away. Dad is livid. We won't stop until we've found them.'

Lewis felt suddenly angry. He thought of his mum. Then he imagined his dad's forearms bulging, his face getting redder and redder by the minute. This was something he didn't need right now.

'Laters, Lewis. If you see anything, get Dad to ring us on the mobile.'

Lewis nodded, his anger towards them long forgotten. Walter crunched the gears and sped from the pavement, blowing grey smoke into the darkening sky.

Lewis quickened his pace. All thoughts of the cricket match had gone out of his mind. He needed to get home. He decided to take a short cut across the playing field. That's when he saw it.

Lewis could see the pavilion on the other side. A red hue lit up the trees behind and thick black smoke billowed out of the roof. Small flames shot up, sending sparks like fireworks.

'Oh no! The pavilion!' he cried out. 'It's on fire!'

22

Lewis saw smoke, pale against the gathering darkness. Sneaky little orange-red flames spurted out of the roof while the thick smoke poured from underneath the veranda floor. Lewis could feel the heat as he drew near. He coughed as a thick cloud of grey smoke lurched towards him, caught by the breeze.

'Stay back! The firemen will be here soon!' warned a voice behind him.

He saw movement away to his right. Several other people were already scurrying about on the scene. He recognised some of them as players from Clifton Seniors. They could only watch as the fire crackled and roared, gathering strength. It had already taken hold of the central part of the building and licked hungrily at the wooden roof. The smoke suddenly engulfed Lewis, stinging his eyelids. He rubbed them with his sleeve, which now smelt of smoke.

He heard a snap and the sound of splitting wood followed by several cracks, like a cap gun. The heat was now unbearable, but Lewis just stood there. He couldn't do a thing to stop it.

'Lewis? What are doing here?'

A hand clasped his shoulder and he spun round in surprise. It was Coach Riley.

'What happened here?' he asked, looking wide-eyed at the fire.

'I don't know. I was just walking home when I saw it.' Lewis could hardly speak for coughing.

'Who would do such a thing?'

.

Lewis looked back at Coach Riley, not knowing what to say. In the rapidly dimming light, Lewis could only make out shapes. He wished he was anywhere but here.

'My God! The whole place is going to go up,' someone from the gathering crowd said.

'I bet it was kids, torching the place,' muttered someone else.

Lewis could hear sirens in the distance. Suddenly, a huge explosion shook the night air and flames leapt up into the sky

'Crikey! The grounds man left petrol for the mower in there,' someone shouted.

At this, everyone moved swiftly back.

Coach Riley pushed Lewis farthest from the crowd.

'Lewis, best keep your head down.'

Two fire engines burst onto the field and in no time at all began tackling the blaze. Lewis saw people moving against the smoke as the engines' lights lit up the powerful jets of water. The firemen had already placed a cordon around the pavilion in an effort to push back some of the onlookers. They were naturally worried about gas leaks and the possibility of huge explosions.

Coach Riley stood stiffly with his hands in his pockets, staring at the fire. Two other men stood beside him; Lewis recognised them from the club. He stood as close as possible, daring not to say anything. Coach Riley glanced over at Lewis but said nothing, then began talking with the two men.

Lewis had an uncomfortable feeling, like someone was talking about him behind his back. For some reason floods of guilt rushed over him. The men from the club seemed to have closed ranks. He really wanted to go over and say something, but as soon as he had plucked up enough courage they had gone, walking alongside a fireman into the darkness.

23

'But it can't be. They've got it all wrong!' Lewis said at the top of his voice.

His dad gave a weak reply from the darkness of the yard. 'Lewis, it's a fact. Not a thing I can do.'

Lewis slammed his foot against the corrugated iron wall that ran alongside the fence. The dogs started barking.

'Chico, Bruno, quiet!' Mr Duckworth shouted.

Lewis smelt tobacco. His dad had started smoking again. Wisps of smoke disappeared over his head. This was a bad sign; he only ever smoked when he was really worried.

Since arriving home from the pavilion Lewis had

been met by the worst kind of news. He'd expected to see pieces of glass from what was left of the shattered window, but not police telling his dad that Charlie, Walter and the Duggan brothers had been arrested, accused of starting the fire.

Lewis should have realised what was happening at the club. Just one look at some of the players' faces had told the story. Even though he'd had nothing to do with the fire, they probably thought he was part of the problem. This had just made Lewis madder than ever.

'But, Dad, they had nothing to do with it. It was the same kids who broke our windows.'

'You sure about that?' his dad shot back between a drag on his cigarette. 'They were out roaming in their van. What d'ya think the police thought of that, eh?'

'No way. It wasn't them. I saw them. They

wouldn't do that.'

'Look, Son, I don't know what to believe. If they didn't do it, then where are these kids?'

Lewis fell silent. He knew it was hopeless. Their family were easy targets, ripe pickings for the police. He saw his dad slump down onto the chalet steps. His body, usually so large and powerful, looked small and hunched. His dream now seemed a long way off.

Lewis knew then that the family's future in the town was bleak. He also realised that with his brothers accused of burning down the pavilion, he would no longer be welcome at Clifton Maidens. His chances of playing in the final were as good as finished.

24

'It just doesn't make any sense,' Lewis said. He was practically in tears. 'I saw them that night. They were looking for some kids. Why would they want to burn down the pavilion?'

'Perhaps,' said Matt with a sigh, 'someone wanted to make it *look* like they'd done it.'

Lewis had gone over to see Matt the following evening. The rest of the day had been terrible. His brothers had arrived home in the early hours of the morning looking pale and drawn. They had been charged with arson and destruction of private property. It just so happened that they would be in court to face these charges the day after the final.

When Walter entered the yard he'd cried out so loudly that both families had wanted to know what happened.

'Dad, I promise we had nothing to do with this,' he'd shouted in frustration. 'You know that. We were nowhere near the fire!'

'But why?' asked Lewis, slamming his hand against the bed. He turned to look at Matt. 'I bet the rest of the Maidens think my brothers did it. My name is probably mud right now. There's no way Riley will put me in the team for the final.'

'Coach Riley won't let this affect anything,' Matt said softly.

'How can you say that?'

'Because you had nothing to do with the fire…'

Matt paused and pursed his lips. 'Coach Riley won't hold it against you. He'll pick the team based on performance, and because of that catch you'll be in the team. And that's that.'

'I hope you're right, Matt. I hope you're right.'

25

Lewis switched off the radio and got up. It was time to go. He felt strange. He should have been excited. It was the evening of the Final. There was a shadow of expectation. He didn't even know if he was playing. Would it matter if he was? he thought to himself as he tied his laces on his pumps.

He looked at himself in the mirror. His shoulders and forearms were developing to become thick and strong like his dad's. He tried to flatten out the folds on the arm of his T-shirt. He looked nothing like a cricketer. People in the game took one look at him and frowned. Yet he knew that when he got a bat in his hand or dived to stop or catch a ball, everything about the way he looked would be forgotten. Coach Riley had seen that. It didn't matter that he didn't wear the right gear. Appearances meant nothing. He just hoped he would get another chance.

He was just about to leave the chalet when he saw a note on the kitchen table.

Good luck tonight, Lewis!

The whole family is rooting for you. I wish I could come and watch, but I need to work tonight. We must carry on and stay strong. Do your best – that's all I ask and you'll make the family proud.

Love always,

Dad

Lewis scrunched up the note and put it in his pocket. This seemed to make him feel worse. His dad was trying to be his typical self, carrying on as if nothing was wrong. But right now everything *was* wrong.

Lewis was more concerned about the reaction from his teammates than the Inter-Town Twenty Final at Westburn.

26

'Just imagine, the County Pros use these steps when they play here,' Matt said excitedly.

As they trotted down the steps towards the oval of bright-green grass, Lewis should have been just as excited. After all, Matt had been right. Coach Riley had picked him. Since arriving in the changing rooms he had tried to take in the padded benches, the lockers, the vending machines filled with Lucozade and the ultra-modern showers. But he'd soon become aware of his teammates whispering and staring at him. He knew what they had been saying.

They took to the field. Lewis could see Westlake ahead of him talking to a couple of teammates. Every now and then they kept looking back at him. Westlake in particular hadn't been pleased when Coach Riley had announced the team.

'What? But, Coach, what was wrong with the starting line-up for the semi-final?'

'You know very well that Drake is still injured. Parks will keep wicket like before. We need speed and agility in the field; Westburn has some powerful hitters.'

Coach Riley had of course been referring to Lewis. Matt had sidled up to Lewis on hearing the news.

'Told you so. Now go and show 'em what you're made of,' he whispered. 'And don't worry about Westlake.'

But that was the problem. He was worried. He was so worried he found it hard to concentrate.

They took their positions in the field. Lewis, head down, wandered off to Long On. He began thinking about his brothers and the impending court case. All week his dad had been talking animatedly to someone on the phone. Lewis didn't know who, but he had a pretty good idea. The Council. His dad must not be working with them any more. Everything seemed to be falling apart.

'Hey, Duckworth!' Lewis heard Westlake call out, interrupting his thoughts. 'You're not fielding there today,' he said, pointing square of the wicket. 'In the covers.'

Lewis' heart missed a beat. Westlake had put him in the very position he had longed for as a fieldsman. This was the place to be. You had to be good to field there. But Lewis' sense of unease wouldn't go away. It was like he was trapped in a bad dream. He thought about the court case again. Then about his dad and his mum's health, which had worsened. The Duggans looked after her most days now. Lewis' head filled with the worst kinds of thoughts.

He didn't even hear the loud smack as the ball thundered off the bat.

'Lewis! Yours!'

The ball flew past him before he had a chance to move and sailed away to the boundary. The match had started and Lewis hadn't even noticed! Westlake stood with his head in his hands. The bowler swore at him, hands on hips.

Lewis tried to forget and get his mind back into the game. Coach Riley had been right. The Westburn batsmen were powerful. They looked older and bigger than the Clifton players. They hit the ball with such speed and power that no matter how hard Lewis dived or lunged, the ball would be past him in an instant. Westlake's shouts grew more desperate. Sometimes Lewis would deflect the ball into the path of another fielder. His hands would be stinging until the next one came blasting towards him.

Eventually, under the orders of Coach Riley, Westlake moved Lewis to a more concealed position. Maybe it was the stinging that caused it, but when he dropped a catch in the deep, he just wanted the ground to swallow him up.

As they trudged off at the end of the innings, Westburn had posted an impressive 183. Lewis' teammates weren't talking to him. That came as no surprise. But worst of all, even Matt wasn't talking to him now.

27

'That's got to be the worst display of bowling since I've been at Clifton, and that's nearly ten years!'

Coach Riley sat on the large table in the middle of the changing room. With folded arms, his eyes panned the room looking from player to player.

'The bowling was too short, the wicket is just too slow for that. It just sat up for them. They had all the time in the world.' His eyes settled on Westlake. 'Al', you set the field too tight. I warned you that they had some powerful hitters,' he continued whilst Westlake sat looking at the floor. 'You attacked too soon. Once they had broken the in-field it was four every time. You didn't have enough covering the boundary...'

Westlake wasn't the only person with his head down. As Coach Riley went on, Lewis looked down at his green-stained trousers. He wiped his hands on them. He felt a stinging sensation across his palms. They were cut and blistered in between the fingers and covered in red dye from the cricket ball.

'...As for the fielding, well, that wasn't much better. It seemed some of you found it difficult to concentrate out there.'

Lewis could almost feel Coach Riley's eyes burning into the top of his head when he said this.

'Right, remember, if this was a football match, it would only be half-time. You've still got a mountain to climb, but your strength this season has been your batting. Al', we'll need a captain's innings from you today.'

Lewis managed to sneak a glance at Westlake. He was playing with a batting glove whilst gritting his teeth. He looked like someone under pressure. Lewis suddenly felt bad. He hadn't helped much. He could see how desperately Westlake wanted to beat Westburn.

Lewis remembered the note from his dad. He had talked about pride and doing his best. Well, so far his best hadn't been good enough. He just hadn't got his mind in gear.

'Right, you lot, get out there and show Westburn why we are the best bunch of under-13s in this town.'

It felt like a team talk any football team would have been given in the circumstances. Coach Riley clapped loudly and gave Patterson and Parks high fives like he was a teenager himself.

As he left, Lewis tried to catch Matt's eye, but he

had turned away to start padding up. Lewis was down to bat at number ten. He doubted he'd play any further part in the match.

It seemed all he could do was watch like every other spectator in the ground.

28

There was still five minutes to go until the restart. Some of the Westburn players had gathered on the benches at the front of the pavilion.

Inglewood spoke first. 'Right, lads, this is it. Keep it tight and the Cup will be ours again.'

'We've got loads of runs to play with. It should be a doddle,' said the boy sitting next to him, instantly receiving a thump on the arm for his troubles.

'That kind of talk will make us sloppy. We need to be hard into them straight away. They've got Westlake, remember.'

'You should be able to deal with him, shouldn't you, Josh?'

'Westlake wants to make up for last season. He'll be tough. Bowl at his legs, that should keep him quiet.'

The boy stopped rubbing his arm. 'What about that Duckworth kid? I heard he's a good bat.'

'Him? You must be joking! Where did you hear that?' Inglewood said, shaking his head. 'I don't even know why he's still allowed to play. That family of his are nothing but trouble. They should be run out of town after what they did and take their stinking mess with them.'

'You mean the fire? It was his brothers that caused it, wasn't it?'

'Believe what you want. They should have been more careful, driving around at night like that. What do they expect? Who cares if it happened to be the other kids from the estate? Just one call, that's all it took.

People from this town don't like that lot from Kings – they should knock it down and run the scum out. All they needed was a reason to get rid of them. And I gave it. They'll be found guilty and that'll be that. No one threatens me and gets away with it,' Inglewood said, feeling his nose tentatively.

'Wow! You mean they didn't do it?' The boy looked wide-eyed at Inglewood. Then came the thump on the arm again. 'Ow! That hurt!'

'You keep your mouth shut or you'll get more of the same. That includes you two as well. If it means getting rid of another family from that cesspit in order to clean up our town, then so be it. And the sooner the better. I bet they encouraged those kids on the estate anyway.'

Lewis got up from the edge of the pavilion where

he'd slumped down intending to watch the rest of the match alone. He breathed in and out heavily, his blood boiling like venom waiting to be unleashed.

He had heard everything.

Lewis appeared round the corner of the pavilion, his body coiled ready to fight. He wanted to drive his fist into Inglewood's soft, fat nose again. The Westburn players had got up and started to make their way onto the field. Lewis continued marching along the pavilion, his eyes fixed on Inglewood. That's when he saw Coach Riley ascending the steps towards him, blocking his way onto the field.

'Lewis, why aren't you with the rest of the team?' he asked, pointing brusquely to the balcony above.

Lewis found himself being stared at by Coach Riley. He didn't flash his usual cool smile.

'Go on, get over there. Support your team,' he said,

emphasising the last three words.

'Sorry, Coach. I was…'

But Lewis couldn't find the words. His mind flashed back to the note from his dad. This was no way to make his family proud. Coach Riley had given him the chance. He couldn't let him down.

By the time he reached the others, the rage he felt had been replaced with a bubbling anger. He sat quietly a few spaces away from the rest of the team. Despite the situation, most of them looked relaxed and sat with their feet up, clearly enjoying the privilege. His body lapsed into some kind of numbed shock as he confined himself to a comfortable chair. His feet were stuck firmly to the floor.

He sensed one or two furtive glances from his teammates, but no one said anything. Lewis watched

Inglewood from a distance. He felt nothing but hatred for him. He knew it would be his word against his if he went to the police. Who would they believe? Not Lewis' for sure. He could try to speak with Coach Riley, but he seemed too caught up in the game; perhaps after the match. But then what could he do? He sighed inwardly. The situation seemed hopeless.

Everything seemed hopeless, even the match. How on earth could he influence the outcome batting at number ten?

30

Lewis tried to focus on the cricket. Westlake was playing well. He fended off Inglewood and scored off the others. The runs came freely and soon Clifton had gone past fifty for the loss of only one wicket after just six overs. They were up on the run rate. Each time Westlake hit a boundary he was greeted by cheers and loud clapping from the balcony. Clifton was making a fight of it.

'If we win from this, it will be a competition record!' Patterson said.

Lewis was amazed at how positive everyone seemed. Clifton had made a great start, and there was still hope. Matt who had been batting really well with

Westlake suddenly found his off stump leaning back at forty-five degrees. He stormed back to the pavilion, scowling back at the bowler from time to time. Lewis had never seen Matt so angry, and as he went trotting past he slammed his bat against a bench.

'I say, hey, young man, calm down there!'

Matt found himself face-to-face with a stiff-looking gentleman in a smart blazer. Lewis could sense the pressure beginning to build.

'Well played, Matt, hard luck, mate,' Patterson said as he put on his gloves and set off for the middle. 'I'll try to keep it going.'

At least he tried, and straight away he hit an edgy four over backward point but was caught next ball at mid-off. Three down. Suddenly, with the loss of two quick wickets things didn't look so good. Next man in was Will Jacobs, who went straight on the attack, placing an off-drive between the bowler and mid-off.

'Shot!' cried Patterson, clapping.

He had come straight back up to the balcony. He was still padded up. He still wanted everything for the team. Westlake was making every effort to push the score along. A fierce pull went for four and then he played a classical forcing shot off the back foot through extra cover. Westburn's off-spinner came on and Jacobs cracked two fours in succession. Lewis could see Inglewood staring, hands on hips.

Lewis found himself clapping fiercely with the others as another boundary signalled the hundred up. He glanced at the scoreboard. They still needed just over eighty runs to win with a little less than ten overs to go. There was another cheer. He returned to the action in the middle. Another wicket. Jacobs caught behind. Five minutes later another Clifton batsman made the long walk back to the pavilion.

'You'd better hurry and get padded up, Lewis,' Patterson said, biting his nails.

Lewis had been playing the part of supporter so well he'd almost completely forgotten he was still playing. By the time he returned to the balcony fully padded up, the call came.

'Lewis, you're in!'

31

'Just give me the strike and I'll do the rest. Just hold up your end, okay?' said a red-faced Westlake as he met Lewis on the edge of the square.

The instructions were clear. But he'd caught the look in Westlake's eyes, that look of defeat. He'd been unable to hide the fact that the situation seemed hopeless. The scoreboard told the story. A mini collapse had occurred. Clifton still needed nearly sixty runs to win, with two wickets remaining and just five overs left.

Lewis took guard. He'd been sat for so long on the balcony his muscles had stiffened. Suddenly thrust into action, his body felt half asleep. He circled his arms once or twice. He blinked and stretched his facial muscles. The light had faded fast. It would be difficult to see the ball well.

The Westburn fielders were noisy and excitable. They sensed victory. From a distance everything had seemed quite sedate. Now, as Lewis prepared to face his first ball, he felt the buzz of intense competition. He crouched low and gritted his teeth. He could hear the pounding of the earth as the bowler began his run.

'Come on, boys, let's send him packing – like the rest of his family.'

Lewis jolted upright. He'd heard Inglewood's sharp voice somewhere behind. Just at the point of delivery, Lewis stepped away from the crease.

'Hey!' The bowler stopped mid-flight as the Umpire's right arm descended down like a parking barrier.

'I'm sorry, I wasn't ready,' Lewis heard himself saying.

'Quack, quack!' Inglewood mimicked.

Lewis stared at Inglewood positioned at backward point. He stood grinning at him. He tightened his grip on the bat handle.

'Boys, can we remain quiet in the field please!' the umpire requested.

The bowler huffed his way back to his mark. This gave Lewis the time he needed. He adjusted his thigh pad and fiddled with his gloves. *Concentrate*, he told himself under his breath. He had to forget Inglewood for the time being; losing his cool wouldn't be good for him or his team.

The bowler was in again, and this time Lewis

played the ball. It was a full delivery slower than he'd expected, aimed at his legs. Twisting his body he was able to angle the bat and glance the ball behind square on the leg side. The ball ran away into space, and a fielder immediately gave chase.

'Run!' Lewis shouted. Even though it wasn't even his call, he'd seen the ball trickle away.

He ran the first one fast and as he reached the bowler's end a quick glance over his shoulder told him that the fielder still hadn't gathered the ball. He turned for a second run. It was only when he was halfway down the wicket that he realised to his horror that Westlake was still entrenched at the other end.

Lewis was about to be run out.

32

'No! Get back, Duckworth!' Westlake screamed, thrusting the palm of his glove towards Lewis.

The fielder had gathered the ball and was about to throw it in. Lewis teetered off balance, still stranded halfway down the wicket.

'Get it in!' The air filled with screams and shouts.

Westburn's fielder fumbled with the ball like it was a bar of soap. Over the course of the next minute a mixture of chaos and confusion reigned.

Amidst the commotion, the fielder panicked. Rather than throwing the ball to the bowler's end, which surely would have signalled the end of Lewis' innings, he threw it towards the keeper, and it also happened to be a terrible throw. Westlake saw what had happened. He didn't want to lose a wicket even if it was Lewis'. It gave him the chance to scamper to the other end whilst Lewis completed his run.

Even worse for Westburn, the wild throw went past the keeper. No one had been backing up. The ball thumped against the advertising hoardings on the far side. The Umpire signalled four overthrows. With Lewis' two runs, that made a total of six runs all off one ball!

Lewis could hear the cheering from the balcony. Then he heard Westlake.

'That was *my* call! What were you playing at?'

Lewis just raised a glove to say sorry. His heart thundered beneath his shirt. His arms already glistened with sweat, his breathing heavy and laboured. He looked about him. He could see that he'd rattled the Westburn fielders. He felt dangerous. His blood was up. He wanted more. He took a deep breath and took up his stance.

The bowler tried too hard with his next ball. Lewis was waiting. This time it was a full toss, and he despatched it with ease over mid-wicket for four. Lewis heard the cheers, louder this time. Ten runs in two balls. Clifton was on the front foot again. He chipped two more runs with the next ball when the umpire signalled the end of the over. Twelve runs off just three balls. If he kept going like that he'd win the match on his own.

Westlake wandered up to him during the changeover.

'Okay, Duckworth, just calm down now, eh? We want to be there at the end and win this thing,' he said as he surveyed the field. 'I'm seeing it like a football now, so just do as I say. No quick singles, okay? Leave the strike to me.'

Lewis nodded. But deep down he couldn't wait to face the strike again. Frustration followed in the next over, as Lewis could only watch as Westlake hogged the strike. By the end of the over a further ten runs had been scored. With just three overs left, they still required thirty-five to win. It still seemed like a tall order.

Westlake waited in the middle for Lewis to reach him at the break.

'Now, it's going to be tough. I was beginning to wonder when they'd bring him on again. He's still got two overs left.'

Lewis looked across at the tall figure rubbing the

ball against his trousers as he passed his short-sleeved sweater to the umpire.

Lewis whispered the name under his breath. 'Inglewood.'

33

'HOWZATT!' Inglewood let out a loud shriek, jumping up and down wildly in front of the umpire.

'Not out,' the umpire said flatly.

Lewis breathed a huge sigh of relief. For the third time that over the ball had fizzed past, narrowly missing both bat and stumps. Westlake grimaced and rubbed the back of his neck. Three missed opportunities. The match was slipping away from Clifton.

As Inglewood walked back to his mark, Westlake chose the opportunity to walk down to Lewis.

'Just hit it! Anything will do, leg, chest, arm, I don't care, and then just run!'

The next ball struck his pad and Lewis ran like

Westlake had asked. It worked; a quick single and Lewis was at the safety of the non-striker's end. He looked away as Inglewood sauntered past him.

'You chicken, Duckworth, scared of a bit of fast bowling.'

Inside he was raging, which is why he'd missed the ball three times. Inglewood had got to him.

'Wait till the next ball. I'll smash you over the sightscreens,' Lewis quipped.

'There won't be a next time, Duckworth,' he said as he ambled back to his mark.

Inglewood launched himself into his long stride. Lewis heard the familiar grunt as he reached the wicket. His front foot slammed down harder than before. It must have been the fastest ball of the day. Seconds later, Westlake's middle stump was cartwheeling behind him.

'Wohaay!' Inglewood whooped.

He drove his fist into the air, running headlong into a mass of ecstatic Westburn fielders.

Lewis looked on, stunned. Westlake couldn't believe what had just happened. He knew it was game over.

34

Lewis' head dropped to his chin. Any last hope of winning the game had gone. Only one man left to come in. He had been a last-minute replacement. Paul Tompkins.

He took guard. His stance looked hunched and awkward. It suddenly dawned on Lewis that Tompkins had never held a bat in his life. Inglewood was like a shark, circling. He could smell Tompkins' fear as he powered in, perhaps for the last time in the match.

Tompkins flinched, closed his eyes and swung. An amazing thing happened. The ball caught the edge of the bat and flew through the slip cordon miraculously for four runs. Lewis smiled. A momentary reprieve perhaps, but at least they were still in it. Two overs to go, thirty runs needed. It still seemed too much to haul back. Lewis knew it was all up to him.

Inglewood couldn't hide his disgust at Tompkins and kicked at the ground, swearing under his breath. He then turned his attention to Lewis.

'I have one more over. If you're still here, Duckworth, you'll get it.'

He couldn't let it worry him for now. He had the next over to play. He knew one mistake and it'd all be over. He relaxed his shoulders and jerked his head level as he waited to face the next ball. It was short of a length. He pivoted onto his back foot at the same time as bringing down the bat with such force that the ball was through the boundary rope before anyone had time to react. The crisp 'clunk' sound meant Lewis had timed it perfectly.

He became oblivious to the cheers from the balcony as the next two deliveries were dispatched with equal measure. He could see the bowler had lost confidence. Bowling short on this track only meant one thing, as Clifton had found out. A mighty six of the fifth ball landed a few steps short of the balcony. He could see his teammates standing and applauding. A clever single of the last ball of the over meant he had protected Tompkins and would face the last over. It was clear to everyone he was the last hope for Clifton.

Just eleven runs needed now as he prepared to face Inglewood for one last time.

35

Lewis brushed the sweat from his face with the smooth pad of his leather glove. He'd been batting for barely twenty minutes, but his T-shirt was soaked through. He could feel blisters forming between his thumb and forefinger. The muscles in his shoulders ached. He'd expended enough energy for two people, most of it through nervous tension.

He could feel the tension amongst the Westburn fielders, too. They weren't as boisterous as before. Some of them looked worried. They still had to get rid of Lewis. He was going to fight all the way. He had clawed Clifton back into the match.

People had spilled out of the pavilion bar onto the boundary edges to watch the thrilling finish. Lewis danced on his toes. He remembered Coach Riley's gruelling coaching session. He needed quick feet to play the right shot to the right ball. His mind churned.

'Eleven off six,' he said to himself. 'Come on…' He could do it. He didn't want to let anyone down.

Then Inglewood arrived at the wicket, muscles straining, veins popping in his neck. He let out a sharp grunt as he released the ball. Lewis' brain clicked into gear. He had barely a tenth of a second to make his decision. Which shot to play? It was a subconscious thought. It was straight and a good length. *Forward defensive*. He moved forward and killed the ball. It bobbled passively back towards Inglewood. Now eleven off five.

Lewis knew he couldn't afford to play wildly. He had to play each ball with merit. He caught Inglewood smiling. There was no doubt that he was the best bowler on both sides. He knew it, too. When he played and missed at the next one, he couldn't contain himself.

'You've got no chance, Duckworth. Face it, you're rubbish!'

Lewis swung wildly at the next one. He could almost hear the groans coming from the balcony. Inglewood had rattled him again. Lewis cursed: eleven off three. The match was slipping away. He'd have to hit a boundary with two of his last three deliveries. He walked away for a moment. *Just relax*, he thought. *Play each shot according to where it pitches.*

Perhaps Inglewood really believed the match was over. His next ball was slower and shorter. He'd become too cocky. Lewis saw his chance. He rose quickly into position and powered it through a gap in the field. He froze his shot. He could almost hear Coach Riley shouting in his ear to hold it. He watched the ball clatter into the advertising hoardings next to the pavilion: seven off two.

Inglewood's face flushed. He looked mad. The familiar grunt returned. The next one was fast. Lewis had to connect with it somehow. It flew down the leg side. He swung hard, but couldn't reach it. He turned to see the ball travel agonisingly towards the keeper. For a moment the ball seemed to hang in the air. As the keeper dived to take the catch, Lewis knew then the match had been lost.

With one ball to go they still needed seven runs to win. Most of the spectators watching from the sidelines had already started to make their way back inside to the lights of the bar.

To toast yet another Westburn triumph.

36

'Wide!' declared the umpire.

He had moved slightly away from the wicket and turned towards the scoreboard.

'What? You must be joking, right?' Inglewood had spun round to see the white-coated figure, arms outstretched.

The umpire, satisfied it had been recorded, turned to face a disbelieving Inglewood.

'It's a wide. Now kindly return to your mark ... no arguments,' he said without a flicker of emotion in his voice.

'How can you call that a wide? He barely missed it!'

Lewis looked on. It seemed harsh. But the facts remained. The umpire had given a wide. The ball wouldn't count in the over. It also meant an extra run. The calculation had changed again: six runs off two balls.

Clifton still had a chance.

Lewis felt a surge of energy. It could be done. He could still hear Inglewood arguing. It brought back horrible memories of school. Lewis had learnt his lesson.

'One more show of dissent and you'll be off!'

It almost sounded like Mr Feltham saying those words.

He watched the Westburn captain put an arm round Inglewood as he returned to his mark. A momentary look at the ball, then he was turning and running again.

Lewis shuffled in the crease, sensing, rehearsing where it would pitch. He heard Inglewood's grunts, louder than ever as his body twisted and arched, actually brushing against the umpire. As if in slow motion Lewis watched the ball travel all the way from his hand. It came short of a length and fast, aiming for his head.

He instantly transferred his weight onto the back foot, chest facing Inglewood. The ball fizzed. He threw everything into it. The red bullet swerved violently in the air, heading towards his face. In an instant he adjusted. Clunk!

He struck the ball cleanly in front of his body, his weight finishing on the front foot. A perfect pull shot. The sound echoed around the ground. Spectators hesitated on the steps; some had rushed back to gather at the boundary's edge. Lewis' arms continued moving, his eyes fixed firmly on the ball as it rose above outstretched arms.

The ball landed safely over the rope. A few spectators jumped out of the way, spilling their drinks. Lewis looked back to see the umpire raise both arms emphatically into the air.

'Six runs!'

He'd done it!

He caught sight of Inglewood, hands on his hips, head bowed. He had nothing to say. No comeback. He'd won the match for Clifton. Without hesitating, Lewis tore the middle stump out of the ground and began heading towards his teammates, dancing down the steps. He could see Coach Riley flashing that huge smile of his. Then he stopped in his tracks.

A little way off to the right of the crowd he could make out three figures walking purposefully towards him. As they grew nearer he recognised one of them as Mr Feltham. He was flanked by two policemen. They didn't appear to be smiling at all.

37

Lewis burst between the scrum of Clifton players that celebrated uncontrollably around him.

'You were brilliant,' said Matt. 'Put it there!'

They exchanged high-fives. Lewis had never been so happy in his life. Then to his surprise, Al' Westlake jumped on his back.

'Champions!' Westlake shouted.

Coach Riley was next in line to congratulate Lewis.

'You showed real grit out there. Held yourself together well.' He flashed his gleaming white teeth. 'You played one for the team, well done.'

He caught sight of Mr Feltham and the two policemen still hovering close by. Lewis felt a hint of irritation. Why did they have to spoil his moment of glory? Why couldn't they just leave him alone? He was convinced Mr Feltham had it in for him.

'Lewis, could we have a word, please?' Mr Feltham called out above the noise.

Lewis pulled himself away from the delighted huddle.

'What is it?'

'It's about your brothers, Charlie and Walter.'

'What about them?' Whatever it was, at that moment Lewis wasn't in the mood to hear it.

Mr Feltham continued. 'Early this morning an attempt was made to set fire to the boathouse on Kingside Lake. The perpetrators were caught. They happened to be kids from the new estate.'

'So?'

'They also admitted to starting the fire at Clifton Park.'

'What? I can't believe it!' Lewis' head was spinning. He couldn't take it all in.

'Your brothers have been released of all charges. The policemen are here to talk to Josh Inglewood. Apparently, his name was mentioned quite a few times when they confessed.'

Lewis couldn't help but laugh, and brought his hand to his mouth apologetically.

'I'm sorry. I'm just so glad.'

Mr Feltham looked at him for a moment. What he said next made Lewis feel even better.

'Well played today, Lewis. I hope I see you at the start of next term, especially when winter nets begin,' he said.

Then out of nowhere Matt and Ben Patterson came storming towards him. They hooked their arms around Lewis' legs and lifted him onto their shoulders.

From his elevated position he could make out Mr Feltham walking towards the pavilion. He nodded at him, and although he couldn't see his face, he could have sworn there was a smile fixed all the way across it.

Lewis was right where he wanted to be. He no longer felt like an outsider. He was on his way.

A week later…

WESTBURN GAZETTE SPORT Friday 28 August

Cricket

DUCKWORTH & WESTLAKE LEAD CLIFTON TO GLORY

Clifton Maidens Under-13s lifted the Inter-Town Twenty Cup at Westburn on Tuesday night and broke the tournament record thanks to match-winning performances by Lewis Duckworth (**37 not out**) and Captain Albie Westlake (**45**). In one of the most thrilling finishes...

Lightning Source UK Ltd.
Milton Keynes UK
UKHW011847210520
363645UK00002B/400